TRUNDLE

P9-DCI-207

MR. BOUNCER'S
HOUSE

FIRE
STATION

BLODGER'S
GATEHOUSE

SIGMUND SWAMP'S
HOUSE & BOATHOUSE

FERNYBANK FERRY

BROCK GRUFFY'S
SHOP

BRAMBLE'S FARM

CHURCH

VICARAGE

RAILWAY STATION

P.C. HOPPIT'S
HOUSE

POLICE
STATION

DR. BUSHY'S
HOUSE

N
W   E
S

This book belongs to:

....

PUBLISHED BY PETER HADDOCK LIMITED, BRIDLINGTON, ENGLAND.
© FERN HOLLOW PRODUCTIONS LIMITED.

CASTAWAYS ON HERON ISLAND

Written and Illustrated by John Patience

It was the morning of the school nature trip. Miss Crisp was taking her class for a visit to Heron Island, which is the little island in the middle of the River Ferny on the Trundleberry Manor Estate.

At Buttercup Cottage the Bouncer Family was in a terrible panic. Patch couldn't find his shoes. They had all hunted high and low without success. "You'll make us late for school," wailed Pippa. "We'll miss the trip." "Don't worry," sighed Mrs Bouncer. "Here they are in the washing basket." "How did they get there?" said Patch. "Oh, I expect they walked!" chuckled Mrs Bouncer. "Come along now, here are your school books. Away you go." She stood at the cottage door and waved them goodbye and off they skipped.

Miss Crisp led her class, walking in pairs, down the dusty, little road to Trundleberry Manor. When they arrived they found Lord Trundle up a ladder inspecting his roof. He came down shaking his head sadly. "The roof is in a terrible state," he said. "In fact, the whole of Trundleberry Manor is in desperate need of repair. Unfortunately I have no money to pay for it! But I don't suppose you want to listen to my troubles. You've come for your nature trip to Heron Island, haven't you?"

Miss Crisp and her class followed Lord Trundle down to the River Ferny where they found a little boat waiting for them. Everyone climbed on board and Lord Trundle cast off and started the engine. "First stop, Heron Island," he cried. The children cheered loudly. They were all very excited. Patch and Pippa peered over the side of the boat down into the dark, green water, where they could see the fish darting around beneath them. Patch thought he caught a glimpse of a big, green pike sliding by. "It was just like a submarine," he said.

From the island, hidden amongst the tall reeds, a strange bird watched the boat approaching. It was Old Man Heron. He was a solitary sort of gentleman

and not at all pleased to have his peace and quiet spoiled by a lot of noisy school-children. He would have to keep an eye on them. He watched as the boat pulled up to the shore and the children and Miss Crisp climbed out. "Have a nice time," said Lord Trundle. "I'll be back to collect you later this afternoon."

"Gather round, children," said Miss Crisp. "Pay close attention now. When we are walking around the island, I would like you to make lists of all the sorts of flowers, birds and butterflies you see. When we get back to school tomorrow we will do some writing about them and make a wall frieze. Stay together now. Off we go!"

The children set off down the woodland path with Miss Crisp leading the way and pointing out things of interest. They were deep in the forest when Patch suddenly tripped over his shoe lace. Pippa giggled. "You did that!" cried Patch. "You tripped me up." "Of course I didn't," replied Pippa. "You did," growled Patch and the next moment they were fighting. Meanwhile Miss Crisp and the rest of the class didn't notice the quarrelling rabbits and continued on their way.

When Pippa and Patch finally broke off from their fighting they realised they had been left behind and ran to catch up. But the pathway split in two directions and they took the wrong one. Soon they were hopelessly lost.

The island suddenly began to seem strange and spooky. The trees appeared more twisty, their branches reaching out as if to grab the frightened little rabbits, and from time to time Pippa and Patch caught sight of Old Man Heron watching them with his black, beady eyes. It was late now and growing rather cold. The two exhausted rabbits took shelter amongst the roots of an old tree.

As they huddled together to keep warm, Patch and Pippa heard a rustling in the undergrowth and out stepped Old Man Heron, looking very severe. "I have been watching you," he said. "You have been very silly. Your teacher and the rest of your class left the island long ago without noticing you were missing." "Then how will we get home?" wailed Pippa. "We are marooned! Castaways!" "Don't worry," said Old Man Heron. "I know a way. Follow me."

Pippa and Patch followed the strange bird to a hollow tree with steps inside it leading down into the earth. "Take this lantern and follow the tunnel," said Old Man Heron. "It will lead you to safety." The rabbits thanked the heron, said goodbye and crept down the steps. The tunnel was narrow and low and seemed to go on for ever but at last it came to an end and there, above their heads, they found a small doorway. Patch pushed it open.

The rabbits climbed through the doorway and found themselves standing in a strange room filled with all kinds of peculiar and interesting objects. There was a rocking horse, a suit of armour, an old painting of a fox cavalier and lots and lots of other things. Pippa found a chest filled with funny old clothes which they both had a marvellous time trying on!

After a time they began to look around for a way out of the room. There was no obvious doorway. "What's this?" said Pippa, pulling a lever in the wall.

Suddenly a panel swung open, revealing a startled Lord Trundle, sitting in his living room. "We're in Trundleberry Manor!" gasped Patch. Lord Trundle was amazed. He had not known about the secret room. "Good gracious!" he exclaimed, noticing the painting of the cavalier. "Do you know, I believe that is 'The Laughing Fox Cavalier'. It was painted by one of my ancestors and has been lost for a hundred years. It is worth a fortune!"

Lord Trundle was perfectly right. He sold the painting to Poppletown Museum and the money more than paid for the repairs to Trundleberry Manor. His troubles were over. As for Patch and Pippa, they had their photographs taken with 'The Laughing Fox Cavalier' by Poppletown newspaper. The headline above the photograph read, "Castaways on Heron Island find Famous Picture".

Fern Hollow

MR. CHIPS'S HOUSE

MR. WILLOWBANK'S COBBLER'S SHOP

MR. CROAKER'S WATERMILL

STRIPEY'S HOUSE

SCHOOL

THE JOLLY VOLE HOTEL

RIVER FERNY

MR. ACORN'S BAKERY

MR. RUSTY'S HOUSE

MR. PRICKLESS'S HOUSE

POST OFFICE

BORIS BLINKS'S BOOKSHOP

MR. TWINKLE'S HOUSE

MR. TUTTLEBEE'S SHOP

MR. THIMBLE'S TAILOR'S SHOP

WINDYWOOD